www.constellate.com

Anansi and the Green Sea Turtles

For more information, please contact:
Constellate Children's Books
Millionaire Street Valley, Virgin Gorda
British Virgin Islands
info@constellate.com

CPSIA Code: PRT0222A
ISBN-13: 978-1-8383326-1-7

Printed in the United States

Anika Christopher

Illustrated by Walden J. Benjamin

In a time when all the trees, flowers, and leaves could still walk, and every wind, wave, and animal could still talk, there was a small village by the sea. In those days, there were no cars, no cities, and no crowds of people. There was just sand where damp footprints were made, a sea with wild crashing waves, and a sky without a moon. The night sky had not always been so dark.

It all began when the villagers refused to honor the moon the same way they honored the sun. This made Nyame, the sky god, so angry that he snatched the moon from the sky. He placed it in a large basket and kept it in the heavens. The villagers begged him to put the moon back, but Nyame refused. He said, “If someone can complete my undoable task, I shall return the moon.” Then, many and many tried, but many and many failed.

One late afternoon, as the light of day began to fade away, a strange wind entered the village. WHOOSH! It was a wind that pushed the sea upon the land. WHOOSH! Up, down, round and round, the wind whirled through the village. WHOOSH!

Gazing out to sea, Anansi the Spider spotted a head above the waves with black, beady eyes staring right at him. “Look, look out there!” Anansi called to the villagers.

Anansi strained his eyes to see who was coming. The villagers looked out.

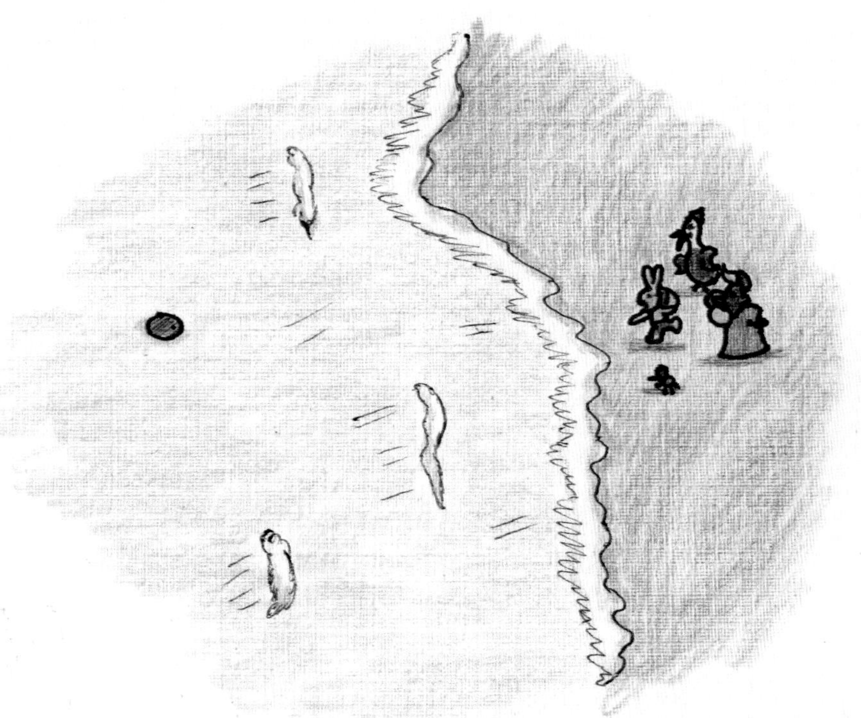

Little by little,
it got closer . . .

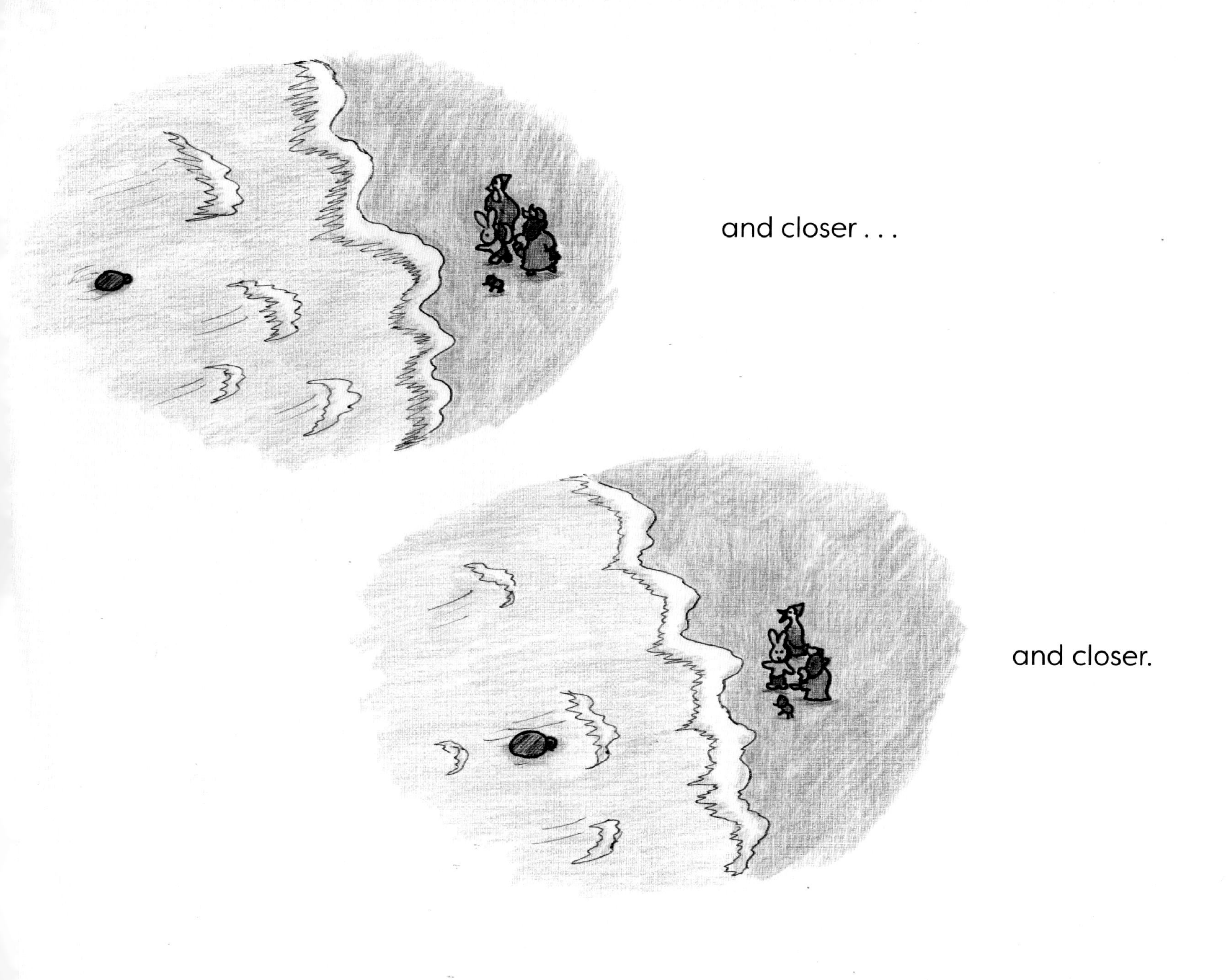

and closer . . .

and closer.

It was an ancient green sea turtle.
"I am Mother Sea Turtle," announced the turtle. The villagers stepped back in surprise. No one had ever seen a sea turtle before.

"Ahh, just as I remember," said Mother Sea Turtle, looking all around. This surprised the villagers because no one knew that Mother Sea Turtle and all the other sea turtles were born on that very beach.
She had now returned to dig her nest in the exact spot where she had been born, as was tradition. But this wasn't so easy to do.

"How did you find the beach without the moon?" asked Anansi.

“When I listen, I hear it. In the wind, I search for the same sound of the breaking waves that I heard on the day I was born. SPLASH! It can still be heard today. SPLASH! The sound is always enough, and when I hear it, I know exactly what it says. It says ‘home.’”

The villagers were amazed. With the villagers at a safe distance, Mother Sea Turtle carefully laid two hundred eggs and covered them in the soft sand.

DIG, DIG, DIG!

"When the moon returns, my baby turtles will hatch, but they must crawl to the water right away," Mother Sea Turtle said. The villagers became very concerned. Without the moon, the baby turtles could easily lose their way and perish.

Before they could say anything else,
it was time for Mother Sea Turtle to go.
"Oh no!" cried Brer Rabbit. "What will
we do? How will the turtles get to the
sea without the moon?"

Anansi had a plan.

The next day, Anansi spun a silken thread all the way to the sky. He climbed and climbed all the way up to the sky kingdom and entered Nyame's court.

"Anansi!" Nyame's voice boomed like crashing thunder, "What is the meaning of this?"

Anansi told the sky god about the baby turtles and how they would need the moon to light their way back to the ocean. Nyame refused. “I will not return the moon until someone does my undoable task.”

"Then I will complete the
task!" said Anansi.

"You, Kwake Anansi, a mere spider, will do the undoable?" Nyame laughed. Many bigger and stronger animals had tried and failed.

The sky god did not believe tiny Anansi could do it.

"Great ruler of the sky, even a spider may do what others cannot," Anansi said.

Nyame thought for a moment.

Finally, Nyame said, "Well then, Anansi, I will let you try." He told Anansi the task, and then Anansi quickly returned to Earth.

"How did it go, Anansi?" asked the villagers.

"We must capture Mmoboro the Stinging Jack Spania," answered Anansi.

No one had ever captured Mmoboro. All who tried had been faced with a terrible thing; a thing so terrible that if I were to just tell you what it was, your face would drain of its color, the hair on your skin would fly up, and you would shake all over in terror.

"Oh no!" cried Brer Rabbit, "What will we do? How will we capture Mmoboro the Stinging Jack Spania?"

Anansi had a plan.

The next day, Anansi got a **BIG** calabash . . .

and he cut a small hole in it.

He then made a plug for the hole and climbed the coconut tree in his yard to tie the calabash at the top.

Anansi's tree bore big coconuts, and there wasn't anything Mmoboro the Stinging Jack Spania loved more than sweet, juicy coconuts. As Mmoboro flew by, Anansi called out to him, "Good day to you! I am giving away coconuts." Anansi told Mmoboro to look up and choose any one he wanted.

"I know you all too well, Anansi. You are full of trickery," buzzed Mmoboro.

"You do not know me," said Anansi, and then added under his breath, "But I do know you." After a short time, Mmoboro was unable to resist the idea of eating sweet coconuts, and he looked up. "Bring this one to me," said Mmoboro.

“What was that?” called Anansi.
“Did you say, ‘Count from one to three’?”
Anansi began to count.
“Nooo, bring this one to me!” said Mmoboro.

“What was that?” called Anansi.
“‘Sing this one high key’?”
Anansi began crooning the
sweetest soca tune.
“NOOO,” cried Mmoboro.
“Bring this one to me!”

Mmoboro was becoming vexed and began to buzz.
Bzzzzz, bzzzzz,
bzzzzz.

“What was that?” called Anansi again. “‘Bring this one to me?’”

“YES!”

Anansi dropped the calabash on Mmoboro. He quickly hopped out of the tree and plugged the hole.

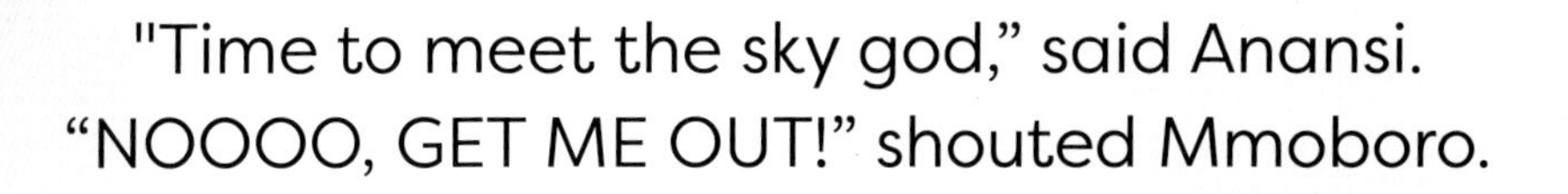

"Time to meet the sky god,” said Anansi.
“NOOOO, GET ME OUT!” shouted Mmoboro.

“Oh, Nyame," said Anansi, bowing. "I am back, and I have Mmoboro the Stinging Jack Spania." Nyame could not believe his eyes.

That very night, the eggs were hatched, but the baby turtles were nowhere to be found.

One late afternoon, as the light of day began to fade away, a strange wind entered the village. WHOOSH! It was a wind that pushed the sea upon the land. WHOOSH! Up, down, round and round, the wind whirled through the village. WHOOSH!

Gazing out to sea, Anansi the Spider spotted Mother Sea Turtle and all her baby turtles.

Soon after that, turtles all over the world were being hatched. They went everywhere. They went all throughout Africa and all throughout the seven continents. And several hundred years later, we are still finding them, thanks to one little spider named Anansi.

The End

ABOUT THE AUTHOR

Anika M. Christopher is a creative writer who lives and works in the Virgin Islands. She is the founder and publisher of Constellate Children's Books. In all that she does, Anika is deeply passionate about the business of telling stories!

ABOUT THE ILLUSTRATOR

At a very young age, Walden J. Benjamin's passion for drawing started at Francis Lettsome Primary School in Tortola, British Virgin Islands. Since then, Walden has honed his skills and is now a visual artist who captures stories and the beauty of the Virgin Islands through his drawings and paintings.